The Boxcar Children Mysteries

THE MYSTERY ON THE TRAIN

created by
GERTRUDE CHANDLER WARNER

Illustrated by Charles Tang

SCHOLASTIC INC.
New York Toronto London Auckland Sydney

ISBN 0-590-56899-X

12 11 10 9 8 7 6 5 4 3 2 1   6 7 8 9/9 0/0 0/1

Printed in the U.S.A.   40

First Scholastic printing, February 1996

Contents

CHAPTER 1

A Special Surprise

"I can't wait until Aunt Jane gets here," ten-year-old Violet Alden said. Violet and her younger brother Benny, who was six, waited by the window. They looked out onto the street for their grandfather's car. He would be bringing Aunt Jane from the airport any minute now.

Aunt Jane was living in San Francisco for a few months so she could be with Uncle Andy, who had to be there on business. She had called a week ago and talked a long time with Grandfather. Then she asked to speak to each of the Alden children. But when she spoke to them, she said, "I won't talk long now. I'm flying from San Francisco to Boston next week and I will see you then. I'll visit you in Greenfield for two days. I have a very special surprise for you."

Since that telephone call, the children had spent a lot of time trying to guess what the surprise would be. Now the special day was here and soon they'd know.

As they waited, twelve-year-old Jessie asked, "I wonder why Aunt Jane would fly all the way across the country to visit for just two days."

"It must have something to do with the surprise," Violet said.

"Maybe the surprise will be cookies," Benny said. He rubbed his stomach. "Last time she brought some special chocolate chip cookies."

"Are you hungry *again?*" Henry, who was fourteen, and the oldest of the children, asked. "You just finished lunch."

Benny glanced at the clock in the hall and

said, "Lunch was at noon. It's two o'clock now."

"I suppose two is the time for chocolate chip cookies," Jessie teased.

"*Any* time is time for chocolate chip cookies," Benny answered.

Henry and Jessie smiled at their younger brother. Benny was always hungry.

Violet left the window and sat down at the table, where she picked up her colored pencils and began to draw. She said, "I am going to keep busy until they get here. That way, I won't be so impatient."

"I really am hungry now," Benny said. "Let's go see if Mrs. McGregor has anything in the kitchen."

"There is an apple pie," Jessie said, "but it's for Aunt Jane's visit. We can't serve it until she gets here."

"I wish she would hurry." Benny sighed.

"Maybe you should find something to do," Henry said. "You need something to take your mind off waiting. You could become an artist like Violet."

The other children looked at Violet, who was working very hard on her drawing.

Benny went over to his sister and asked, "Is that Watch?"

"Yes," Violet said. "I've got the tail and legs right but he moved so much that I couldn't quite make his head look right."

"I think it looks like Watch," Jessie said.

"It looks like a dog all right," Violet agreed. "But I'm not certain it looks like Watch."

"Sure it does," Benny said. "And you've put our old house in the picture."

"Yes," Violet said, "I like to draw our old boxcar. It's easy because it has nice square corners and it never moves."

At one time, after their parents had died, the Alden children lived alone in a boxcar. Then their grandfather found them and brought them home to Greenfield to live with him.

"Here they come!" Jessie said. "There's Grandfather's car."

Violet and Benny rushed to the door. Jessie and Henry followed behind them. They watched as Aunt Jane and Grandfather got out of the car.

"She has just one suitcase," Jessie said. "I guess she really is staying only two days."

Aunt Jane hugged all four children. Then she stepped back and said, "Let me look at you. Yes, you are all growing taller."

Aunt Jane hugged everyone again. They all went into the living room and Henry and Jessie served milk, tea, and pie. After a cup of tea, Aunt Jane said, "About that surprise I promised." Her eyes twinkled.

"Is it here?" Benny asked.

"Yes," Aunt Jane smiled and patted her purse. "In a way, you might say the surprise is here. On the other hand, you might say it's in San Francisco."

"What is it?" Benny asked.

"Can you guess?" Aunt Jane asked. "Your grandfather says you are very good detectives."

"We are," Violet said, "but we can't guess how a surprise you brought us could be here

and in San Francisco at the same time."

"What is it?" Benny asked eagerly again. "We've been waiting all week."

"You've been very patient," Aunt Jane said. She smiled and opened her purse. "Now, children, here is the special surprise."

Aunt Jane pulled out a brown envelope.

"I don't think there is anything good to eat in that envelope," Benny said.

Aunt Jane smiled at her youngest nephew and said, "You will like this surprise, Benny. And it includes good things to eat."

"I can't guess," Benny said. "It's a small envelope."

Aunt Jane opened the envelope and showed them five brightly colored tickets. "These are train tickets. How would you children like to take a train trip with me to San Francisco?"

"Ooh," the children said at the same time. Then they all began to ask questions at once.

"Are we going all the way to California on a train?" Jessie asked.

"Yes."

"Will we sleep in one of those little rooms?" Violet asked.

"Jessie and Violet will share a compartment and Henry and Benny will share another one. Your compartments are called double slumbercoaches. Each slumbercoach has two seats which change into beds at night. I'll sleep in a roomette. It has a nice easy chair for reading and one bed at night."

"Will we *really* be able to sleep in one of those little rooms?" Violet asked.

"Yes, you'll fit just fine. And those little rooms are called compartments. They are quite comfortable," Aunt Jane explained. "You'll have your own toilet and sink in your room. There are showers right down the hall."

"I've always wanted to see how they made those little beds," Henry said.

"The beds are bigger than you think," Aunt Jane said.

"Two beds in those small compartments." Henry shook his head. "I don't know how they do it."

"The beds come down from the walls," Aunt Jane said.

"Where will we eat?" Benny asked.

"In the dining car. It's a restaurant with a cook and good food," Aunt Jane said. "And there's a club car which has a snack bar, too. You'll find plenty of good things to eat."

"Do I get the top bunk?" Benny asked.

"You can take turns." Then Aunt Jane added, "I know you used to live in a boxcar. That's why I was surprised when your grandfather mentioned the last time I was here that you'd never been on a train trip."

"That's right," Henry said. "We lived all those months in a train that never moved."

"Well, these trains move." Aunt Jane laughed.

"It is a wonderful present," Jessie said. "How long will the trip take?"

"We'll cross the whole country in just three days and nights. We're going to go all the way to the Pacific Ocean. That's about three thousand miles. Then you'll visit with Uncle Andy and me for a few days in San Francisco and you can fly home."

Henry asked, "Will the train make stops?"

"Several," Aunt Jane answered. "We actually will travel on two trains. One goes from Boston to Chicago and then we'll change to a second train which takes us to San Francisco. I have a map," Aunt Jane said. She pulled out a large map and put it on the table.

All the children watched as Aunt Jane traced her finger along the map. "We'll travel through cities and farmland, through deserts and two ranges of mountains. This red line shows the route we'll take. We leave Boston tomorrow night and when we wake up, we'll be in Indiana. We have a two-hour stop in Chicago in between trains, so I'll take you to a wonderful German restaurant I know."

Aunt Jane smiled at Benny and brushed her hand across his hair. "Do you like German food? Knockwurst and sauerkraut? Apple strudel?"

Benny looked doubtful as he said, "I think so."

"Aunt Jane?" Violet asked quietly. "Did you say we leave tomorrow?"

"Yes. Your grandfather will drive us to Boston and we'll catch the train at exactly four-thirty."

"Then we'd better start packing," Violet said.

"Pack light," Aunt Jane said. "Remember, those train compartments aren't very large. You may each take one suitcase."

"I'll take all purple clothes," Violet decided. "That way, everything will match. And I'll have plenty of room for my colored pencils and sketching pad. Will there be pretty scenery?"

"Gorgeous," Aunt Jane promised them. "There will be a lot to see."

"Should I pack a lunch?" Benny asked.

"Don't worry, the food is wonderful," Aunt Jane promised him.

"Then I'll only pack a box of crackers and a bag of cookies. Just for emergencies," Benny said with a smile.

CHAPTER 2

Trouble on the Platform

The next day, Grandfather drove them to the train station in Boston. The train station was very large and confusing. People rushed about in all directions and many announcements came over the loudspeakers at the same time. The Aldens stayed close to Aunt Jane as they walked through the crowded station.

Violet said, "I'll bet there are people from all over the world in this train station. I didn't know so many people took trains."

"Yes," Aunt Jane answered. "Some of

them live in places where it is easier to take a train than to fly. Others don't like to fly. Some people make train riding their hobby. They travel on every railroad in the United States at least once."

"That sounds like a good hobby," Benny said. "Maybe I'll do that."

"This is a long walk," Violet said. "I'm glad my suitcase is small."

"I'm getting tired, too," Benny agreed. Then he looked at the sign on the platform. "Uh-oh! We have to go all the way back inside the station."

"Did you forget something?" Aunt Jane asked.

"No," Benny answered. "But the sign says Chicago. We're going to San Francisco."

"We *change* trains in Chicago," Aunt Jane reminded him. "This is the right train. The Lake Shore Limited. It's a single-level train. In Chicago we change to a double-decker train called the *California Zephyr*."

Benny laughed. "I'm glad we're in the right place. My suitcase is too heavy to go all the way back and try again."

"Let's wait right here until the conductor tells us we can board. These are the sleeping cars," Aunt Jane said.

"How do you know?" Henry asked.

"See if you can guess," Aunt Jane answered.

Henry studied the train for a few minutes and then he said, "These cars have smaller windows, don't they?"

"Exactly," Aunt Jane said.

Suddenly the children heard a loud voice shouting, "You can't have it!"

They turned and saw a young woman with bright red hair. A taller, older woman was pulling at something large and black that the girl was holding. They were pulling very hard in opposite directions.

The older woman said, "Let go! I will *not* permit you to take them."

"They're mine!" the younger red-haired woman answered in a very loud voice.

Just then, the conductor called, "All aboard. All aboard."

"I wonder what they're fighting over?" Violet asked.

Jessie said, "They sound really angry. It looks like they're fighting over that suitcase."

"It's not a suitcase," Violet said. "It's an artist's portfolio. It's built especially so artists can carry big drawings and paintings."

"Do you think the young woman is the artist?" Jessie asked.

"Maybe she's trying to take the older woman's paintings?" Henry suggested.

Benny turned to Aunt Jane and said, "See, we aren't even on the train and we've found a mystery."

"But we must get on the train now," Aunt Jane said. "The conductor has called twice."

"Look!" Henry said. Just then the younger woman gave the portfolio a big tug. She pulled so hard that the older woman fell down. The younger woman looked frightened and started to walk toward the older one. Then she seemed to change her mind. She quickly grabbed her suitcase and the portfolio and jumped onto the train.

Henry ran over to the older woman and helped her up on her feet. He asked, "Are you all right?"

"Yes, of course," the older woman said. "I just lost my balance."

"Are you sure you're not hurt?" Henry asked. "Do you want us to call the conductor or someone?"

"I'm fine," the older woman said sharply.

"Did that girl take your portfolio?" Henry asked.

"No!" The older woman shook her head. "It was her portfolio. And I don't need any help!" She turned her back on Henry and walked quickly away.

When Henry returned to his family, he said, "She's all right. She says the portfolio belongs to the girl."

"It was nice of you to help," Aunt Jane said. "But we *must* get on the train now."

"The red-headed girl won the tug of war," Jessie said thoughtfully. "I hope the portfolio really is hers."

The Aldens boarded the train and the conductor directed them to their sleeping car. The girls were in room 102 and the boys were across the hall in room 105. Benny opened the door and said, "Wow! this really *is* a small room! Where do we put our suitcases?"

Then he saw a doorknob beside the sink and opened it. "This is a closet," he said. "We can put our suitcases in here." They stowed their suitcases in the little closet and tried out the sink.

Then Benny went across the hall to visit his sisters. The girls were looking out the window at the platform. Jessie pointed. "The woman who fell down is still standing on the platform."

"What's she doing?" Benny asked. He looked out the window. Then he answered his own question. "She's talking to one of the conductors."

Henry joined them. He couldn't quite fit into the compartment, but he stood in the corridor and scrunched down so he could see out the window. "He's a porter," Henry said. "The conductor is the one who says when to get on and off the train. The porters carry bags and help you."

"She's giving him money," Jessie reported to the others. "It looks like a lot of money."

"Maybe she's buying a ticket," Violet suggested.

"No," Jessie said. "She can only buy a ticket at the ticket booth."

The children watched as the porter boarded the train and the older woman stood alone on the platform.

"Why would she give the porter money when she's not even getting on the train?" Violet wondered.

"She looks sad," Jessie said. "I wonder what the argument was all about."

"When I offered to call for help, she looked sort of strange," Henry said.

"I wonder why they were fighting over the port . . . port . . ." Benny couldn't say the new word.

"Portfolio," Violet said. "The red-headed girl looked young. Maybe she's an art student."

"Maybe," Henry said. "But let's not waste our time talking about that. Let's explore the train."

"Good idea," Benny agreed.

"We can all take a look around," Violet agreed. "Maybe we'll meet the art student somewhere."

"Maybe in the snack bar," Benny suggested.

The Alden children went out into the corridor and found Aunt Jane's compartment. "We're going to explore," Benny said. "Do you want to come along?"

Aunt Jane shook her head and said, "You children can look around while I read. But be sure to save some room for dinner."

"Don't worry, I would never miss dinner," Benny promised her.

CHAPTER 3

Meeting Annie

As the Aldens explored the train, they found out it was very long. The children counted twenty cars. On one end were the sleeping cars and on the other there were many coach cars with big, comfortable seats. The porters were handing out pillows. "A lot of people sleep all night sitting up in the seats," Jessie said. "We're lucky we have beds."

"I'll bet those big seats are pretty comfortable," Benny said. "But I like our slumbercoaches."

They loved walking from car to car and feeling the way the floor rolled beneath them. Benny said, "It's a little like sailing, isn't it?"

"Not really," Henry said thoughtfully. "It's more like flying in an airplane, I think."

"I think it's exactly like riding in a train," Jessie said, laughing.

They walked all the way to the end of the train and turned around. On their way back, they stopped to look at the club car. The club car had tables and chairs and, at one end, there was a snack bar where a woman was selling drinks and snacks. "Let's sit here," Henry said. He pointed to an empty table with four chairs.

"I think I'll have a snack," Benny said.

"Just get a drink for now," Jessie said. "It's almost time for dinner."

Benny smiled at the thought of dinner and looked out the window of the club car. He said, "I know we're moving and the trees are standing still. But when I look out the window, it seems as if the trees are running away."

Benny got a drink and they sat and

watched the people parade through the train. The train was filled with people of many ages and some were quite dressed up. Others wore jeans and T-shirts or sweaters. There were four women who were playing cards at a table next to them. Other people were talking or reading. Some stared out the window at the darkening sky. Everyone looked very relaxed.

A woman in uniform came through ringing a bell and singing out, "First call for dinner."

"We'd better go," Henry said. "Aunt Jane is waiting for us."

"I wonder what dinner will be like," Jessie said.

"Let's get Aunt Jane and go and see," Benny said.

When they returned, Aunt Jane was sitting in her little compartment reading. She asked, "Well, did you see everything?"

"Not everything," Jessie admitted. "It is a very long train."

"We saw a lot," Benny added. "We saw the coach cars and the snack bar in the club car." Then he added, "Is it time for dinner yet? I'm hungry."

Aunt Jane laughed and said, "I suppose we can go to the early seating. Then you might want to watch the sunset from the dome coach."

"Where is the dome coach?" Henry asked. "We missed that."

"The dome coach is the only two-story car on this train," Aunt Jane explained. "We have to climb some stairs and then there's a coach that has a glass roof. We can watch the sunset and the stars."

"That sounds great!" Violet said.

The dining car was almost full when they got there. Henry said, "The tables only hold four people. We'll have to split up."

"That will be fun," Jessie said. "We can meet new people."

Violet and Aunt Jane sat with a young couple. Benny, Jessie, and Henry were joined by a man who was all alone. He was a slender, dark-haired man with a dark beard. He was wearing sunglasses.

"Is this your first train trip?" Benny asked the man.

He nodded his head but said nothing.

Benny thought he had better not ask any more questions, since the man didn't seem to want to answer.

There were menus on the table and Benny looked his over carefully. When the waiter came by to fill his water glass, he said, "I'll have a hamburger, please."

"You must write out your order," the waiter explained. He showed Benny the order pad and pencil. "First, circle your drink choice," the waiter said.

Benny circled milk and then he wrote down the word "hamburger." He handed his order to the waiter and said, "I've never had to write down an order before."

"Trains always ask you to write down your choices," the waiter explained, smiling. "It saves a lot of trouble."

"It's a good idea," Benny said.

The others all wrote down spaghetti with meatballs. Then Benny said, "I bet they have you write everything down because of the noise."

"It is noisy," Henry agreed.

"I like the sound," Jessie said. "It sounds like the wheels are singing."

Very soon, the waiter came back with their orders and Henry, Jessie, and Benny started eating their dinners. When they were about halfway through, the man at their table stood up and nodded, then left.

"He didn't eat much," Jessie observed.

"I think he was having trouble with his beard," Henry said. "He seemed to let it get in his way when he tried to chew."

"Maybe it was a new beard," Jessie said.

"It takes a while to grow a beard that long," Henry said. "I don't think it could be too new."

"Why do you think he was wearing sunglasses?" Benny asked.

"Maybe he's a famous movie star and doesn't want to be recognized," Jessie said.

When dinner was over, Violet came over to their table and sat down at the empty place. She said, "That was fun. Now we have two new friends. Mr. and Mrs. Wilson were married last week and they're going to visit her mother in Madison, Wisconsin. They were very nice. What was the man who sat with you like?"

"We don't know. He didn't say a word," Henry said.

Jessie added, "I had a hard time not laughing. His beard kept getting into his soup."

"That's probably why he was so quiet," Benny said. "I'm glad I don't have a beard to get in my way when I eat dinner."

"He *was* sort of strange," Henry said.

"I wonder what happened to that art student," Violet said. "Do you think we'll see her again?"

"Probably," Jessie said.

"Maybe not," Henry said. "It's a big train."

"I guess we'll just have to wait and see," Violet added. "Let's go find the dome coach and watch the sunset."

The four children made their way through the cars until they came to the dome coach. They climbed the stairs to the second story and looked around. There were many chairs and two sofas arranged so that they looked out of the big open windows.

The chairs on the side of the sunset were all filled so the children stood as they watched a big red sun sink below the city buildings. "I wonder where we are," Henry said. "I have a map but I'm not sure if we are still in Massachusetts or New York state. I'll ask the conductor."

"I don't know where we are now," Jessie answered. "But Aunt Jane says when we wake up in the morning we'll be in Indiana."

The sun was almost completely gone. There was just a small red stripe behind the trees they were passing. Benny said, "I'm sleepy. Is it time to go to bed yet?"

"Not quite," Henry answered. "Are you really sleepy or do you just want to see how our room turns into a bedroom?"

Benny smiled and said, "I think it will be fun to sleep on the top bunk. Can tonight be my turn?"

"Sure," Henry answered, "but it is too

early to go to sleep. Want to walk around some more?"

"Let's stay here," Violet said quickly. Then she whispered, "That red-haired art student is over there. I'd really like to talk to her."

They all looked in the direction Violet pointed. The young woman they'd seen on the platform was sitting in a chair at the end of the observation car. Henry said, "She *is* drawing. Maybe she really is an art student."

"I guessed right," Violet said. "Does she have her portfolio with her?"

"No. Just a sketch pad."

"I'm going to talk with her," Violet said. Violet went over and sat down in the empty chair beside the red-haired young woman. She didn't seem to notice Violet and kept right on working on her drawing.

Violet sat for a while and then she said quietly, "I'm Violet Alden. I'm an artist, too."

The young woman looked up and smiled. She said, "I'm Annie Perkins. I'm not really an artist but sketching is my hobby."

"Were you sketching the sunset?" Violet asked.

"No." Annie shook her head. "It is too difficult to draw landscapes from a moving train. Besides, I like to sketch people. I was sketching that woman over there." Annie nodded her head slightly.

"May I see?" Violet asked.

Annie passed the sketchbook over to Violet. Violet looked at the drawing and then at the woman. "It's great, it looks just like her."

"That's because she's got a long nose," Annie said. "It's easy if people have at least one unusual feature."

Violet and Annie began to talk about drawing. "I like to draw noses," Annie said. "I usually get them right. The hardest parts of people are their chins," Annie said.

"Yes," Violet agreed. "Noses are easy. But my favorite thing to draw is ears. I'm very good on ears."

"Are those your brothers and sister over there?" Annie asked.

"Yes," Violet answered.

"Why don't you ask them to come over?" Annie said.

Henry, Jessie, and Benny joined Violet and Annie and everyone introduced themselves.

"Do you have other sketches with you?" Violet asked. "I would love to see some of your other work."

"Yes," Jessie agreed.

"I only have the one drawing," Annie said.

"We saw you carrying a large portfolio when you got on the train," Henry said. "Do you have your artwork in that?"

Annie shut her sketchbook quickly and said, "Those drawings don't count. They're old."

"I'd love to see even the older things," Violet said. "I'll bet I could learn a lot from you."

Annie seemed very nervous as she said, "I don't have any other sketches to show."

"Oh, well, we'll have lots of sketches by the end of the trip," Violet said.

"We're going to see my Uncle Andy in

San Francisco. His wife, Aunt Jane, gave us this train trip as a special surprise. Where are you going?" Jessie asked, trying to change the subject. It was clear Annie didn't want to talk about her portfolio.

Annie smiled quickly and said, "I'm going to San Francisco, too. Now that I'm out of high school, I can live wherever I want. I'll go to art school in San Francisco and live with my Uncle Bob there."

"Was that woman on the platform your grandmother?" Henry asked.

Annie flushed. "You saw the quarrel on the platform? That was my Aunt Ellen. She's really my great-aunt. My parents were killed five years ago in a car crash and I've been living with her. But now I'm going to live with my father's youngest brother — Uncle Bob."

"Your aunt seemed very upset," Violet said gently.

Annie said, "I guess she was upset that I was leaving. But I need to live my own life. My aunt doesn't want me to go to art school. She tried to take my portfolio from me so I wouldn't have anything to show. Then the art school wouldn't let me in."

The Aldens noticed that Annie's face was flushed and she was looking down at her sketchbook as she said this. Annie stood up, said good night, and quickly left the dome coach.

Then Jessie said, "I think all that talk about Annie's aunt upset her."

"Yes, she seems unhappy about something," Violet said. "When I asked to see her work, she seemed quite nervous."

"Maybe the portfolio doesn't have art in it at all," Benny said.

"It's very big but thin," Jessie said. "Not much else would fit in a portfolio."

"There is *something* in there that both women wanted," Henry said. "That was quite a tug-of-war on the platform."

"It could be stuffed with stolen jewels," Benny said. His eyes lit up.

"Annie's not a jewel thief," Violet said quickly. "She's just a young art student who is moving from Massachusetts to California.

If she says she has her artwork in her portfolio, I believe her."

"If the artwork is only Annie's then it can't be valuable," Henry pointed out. "She's just a student."

Violet shook her head and said, "Annie was really nice. Just because she seemed nervous doesn't make her suspicious. But you know, I do think she's upset about something more than leaving her aunt."

CHAPTER 4

Changing Trains

The Boxcar Children watched the night sky and talked about their first day on the train until it was time to go to bed. Then Henry said, "Let's hurry. I really want to see how they turn that compartment into a bedroom."

They walked quickly through the train and when they got to their car, they saw Annie standing in the corridor right next to Aunt Jane's room. "Hello, Annie," Violet said. "Is your room in this car?"

Annie seemed very friendly again. She said, "Yes, I'm right here. I guess we're neighbors. That's nice."

"Your compartment is right next to Aunt Jane's," Benny told her. "We're down the hall. Our rooms are opposite each other. I'm going to sleep on the top bunk."

"That sounds like fun," Annie said. "I'm waiting for the porter to finish making up my room."

Just then, the porter backed out of Annie's room and said, "It's all ready to go, Miss." He was carrying her portfolio.

Annie reached for the portfolio quickly and said, "That's mine."

"It's too big for your compartment," the porter said. "I'll put it in the baggage car."

"No!" Annie said. She grabbed the portfolio from the porter and took it into her compartment. Then she quickly shut the door.

The porter shrugged and turned to make up the girls' room. As the Aldens stood in the corridor waiting for him to finish, Benny whispered to the others, "That's the same porter that we saw the older woman give money to earlier."

Jessie nodded. "Maybe whatever is in that portfolio *is* really valuable, after all."

"Maybe Annie's aunt paid the porter to take care of the drawings," Henry said. "Or maybe she paid him to return the portfolio to her."

The porter popped his head out of the compartment and smiled. He was a tall, good-looking man. He said, "Hi, my name is Vincent."

Each of the Aldens introduced themselves and they watched as Vincent tucked in the sofas and table and pulled the beds down from the walls. As he pulled down the two top bunks, Henry asked, "Will Annie be able to store her portfolio on her top bunk?"

"Annie?"

"The young red-haired woman whose room you just made up," Jessie said.

"We saw you talking to Annie's aunt on the train platform," Henry said.

"You mean back in Boston? Was she the

red-haired girl's aunt?" Vincent answered easily. "I figured it was her grandmother. She asked me to watch out for the girl. I think she thought she was too young to travel alone." Vincent smiled and said, "She'll be fine, though. Not much can happen on a train."

"Those your sketches?" Vincent asked Violet. He picked up her sketchbook and looked through it. "You've got a lot of blank pages to fill."

He left the compartment, whistling as he went down the corridor. Soon, every compartment was ready for the night and Vincent moved on into a different car.

"Vincent certainly seems like a nice guy," Jessie said as she and Violet climbed into their beds.

Violet said, "I hope the noise of the train doesn't keep me awake."

"Me, too," Jessie said. "But the way the wheels go round and round is sort of like a song, isn't it?"

"I suppose so," Violet answered.

Within minutes they were all fast asleep.

* * *

The next morning they woke up early and went into breakfast before most people were up. Aunt Jane sat with some other people and the children shared a table. As they ate, they talked about their trip.

"I really like riding this train," Benny said as he put a forkful of pancake in his mouth. "I don't think I want to change trains in Chicago."

"The next train will be even better," Henry promised. "It's a double-decker and we will go through some of the most beautiful scenery in the United States. The brochure says . . ."

"But I like this train," Benny said.

"We *have* to change trains," Henry reminded him. "This one just turns around and goes back to Boston."

Violet saw Annie come into the dining car and waved to her. Annie waved back and sat down at a table directly across from them. She ordered toast and coffee and orange juice.

Henry finished his breakfast of eggs and

potatoes and said, "I'm going to get a time-table from the conductor. Then I'm going to plot the times on our map, so when we look out the window we will know where we are. See you later."

Henry left and Violet suggested that Annie bring her coffee over to their table. When Annie joined them, Violet said, "Henry's our navigator. He is keeping track on our map. He marks down the time and that's the way we know where we are. He's going to do that all the way to San Francisco."

"I can't wait to get to San Francisco," Annie said. "I'm going to enroll in the California Arts Academy. My Uncle Bob says it's one of the best schools."

"Is your Uncle Bob nice?" Benny asked.

"I hope so." Annie looked scared as she spoke. "His letters are really wonderful. My aunt never talks about him so I don't know much — just that he is my father's step-brother."

"So you sort of ran away from home?" Benny said.

Annie shook her head. "Not really. My

Aunt Ellen knew I was going. She was upset but she drove me to the train station."

The Aldens were silent as they remembered the quarrel between the two women on the platform.

After breakfast, they introduced Annie to Aunt Jane. Their aunt invited Annie to spend the time during the train stop in Chicago with them. She said, "Since you are taking the same train we are why not stick together? We're going to walk to a great German restaurant I know. Would you like to join us?"

"I'd love to," Annie said eagerly. Then she added, "But I really can't. I need to stay with my luggage."

"Vincent said he'd put our luggage on the next train for us. He's going to San Francisco also. I'm sure he would be happy to take care of yours as well," Aunt Jane said.

"No, I really must stay with my things," Annie said. "But thanks for asking me."

The Aldens didn't see Annie the rest of the morning. About eleven-thirty, Vincent came to their compartments and loaded their bags onto a cart. "I'll have them all stowed for you on the *California Zephyr*," he promised.

The train pulled into the Chicago station right on time and the Aldens walked up another long platform to the main waiting room of the station. There were lots of people and noise but this trip was easier because they didn't have to carry their bags.

As they walked, Annie came running around the corner and almost knocked Jessie down. "Vincent!" she gasped. "Have you seen Vincent?"

She didn't really wait for them to answer, but ran as fast as she could run down the platform. "Annie's in trouble," Violet called out. "Let's help her." Violet began to run and soon all the other Aldens were running as well.

They came into the huge waiting room and looked all around. There were hundreds of people and many of them wore uniforms like the one Vincent wore. "Look for Annie's red hair," Henry said.

The Aldens stayed together but looked in four different directions. Finally, Benny shouted and pointed, "She's over there!"

Annie was sitting on top of her suitcase, clutching the portfolio in her arms. Her face was flushed and she was obviously out of breath.

The Aldens ran over and Henry asked, "What happened?"

"Vincent took my bags," Annie explained. "I just turned my back for a minute and he loaded my bags onto his cart and took them. I called out but he didn't hear me. I almost lost him."

She was shaking and she held the portfolio close to her. Her face was very red.

"It's his job to move bags," Henry said. "He was probably trying to be helpful."

"Why were you so upset?" Violet asked softly.

Annie looked from one Alden to the other and smiled. "I guess I just got a little excited," she explained. "I expected to carry my own bags and when they were gone, I was really surprised."

Annie looked so upset and worried that Violet had to ask her, "Annie, is something else wrong?"

"Nothing you can help with," Annie said. She wiped her eyes with a handkerchief and looked away.

"Are you crying?" Benny asked. "Can we help?"

"I just have something in my eye," Annie said. "I'm not crying." She stood up, picked up her suitcase and walked slowly away.

The four Aldens and Aunt Jane had a wonderful time walking in Chicago. Since they had plenty of time, they stopped and looked in several shop windows. Each of them bought a postcard to send to Grandfather. Henry and Jessie selected scenes of the tall buildings. Violet chose a famous modern painting from the Chicago Art Institute. Benny chose a postcard of a sailboat and wrote, *"Dear Grandfather, The train feels like a sailboat most of the time. Love, Benny."*

The children enjoyed the German restaurant. Their soda was served in heavy old-fashioned mugs with scenes of Germany on them. They ordered German sandwiches and tried some special dishes. Jessie liked the red cabbage but didn't like the sauerkraut. Henry liked the applesauce and Violet liked the potato pancakes best.

Benny said, "I like German food."

"What did you like best?" Aunt Jane asked.

"Everything," Benny said with a smile.

CHAPTER 5

A Midnight Call for Help

The Aldens and Aunt Jane got back to the train station in plenty of time before the train had to leave. As they walked out onto their track, Jessie pointed and said, "Look, that's Annie over there."

She was still sitting on her suitcase and holding the portfolio tight.

"She looks as if she thinks the portfolio will run away from her," Benny said.

"She is really nervous about it," Henry said. "I wonder what could be in it?"

"Violet asked her," Jessie reminded them.

"She said it was her drawings. But she acts as if it were something a lot more valuable than student drawings."

Henry said, "Violet could be right. Maybe Annie is in some kind of trouble."

"Maybe we should keep an eye on her," Benny suggested.

"If she has a room next to ours like she did last time, it will be easy to keep an eye on her," Jessie said.

"But this is a much bigger train," Henry said. "All the cars are double-deckers. She may not be right next door to us again."

"Wherever she is, I think we should try and stick close," Violet said. "She's my friend and I want to help."

They boarded the *California Zephyr* train and quickly discovered that Annie was not in their sleeping car. Their new compartments were on the bottom floor and there were only six rooms. The Aldens and Aunt Jane took three of them. There was a family of four in the bigger family bedroom at the end of the hall and a woman in a wheelchair at the other end. The one remaining compartment was occupied by an older couple.

"Let's check and see if we can find Annie," Benny said.

"There are several sleeping compartments," Jessie reminded them. "Some are upstairs and some downstairs, so it will be a lot harder to find Annie."

"We'll find her," Violet said. They immediately began to walk up and down the cars looking for Annie, but after about an hour's search, they had to admit that Annie was nowhere around.

"Maybe we will see her at dinner," Henry said. "Or later in the observation lounge."

"Or maybe we can ask Vincent where she is," Benny said.

Dinner that evening was in a much bigger, fancier dining room. The tablecloths were white linen and there were small silver vases with fresh flowers on each table.

"This train trip is really wonderful," Jessie said. "Thank you for inviting us, Aunt Jane."

"I'm glad you like it," Aunt Jane said. "I

want this to be a very special experience for you."

"It is. We like everything," Benny added. "We like our rooms and our beds and the way the train rattles and shakes. This is a great surprise present."

Aunt Jane and Violet sat with another young couple. Henry, Jessie, and Benny sat at a table with a small man who was wearing a dark gray pinstriped suit. He was about the same age as Grandfather and seemed very glad to share a table with the children.

When they sat down, the man stood up and shook everyone's hand and said, "Allow me to introduce myself. Reeves is the name, Herbert Reeves."

The children introduced themselves and then they wrote down their orders for dinner. Henry and Jessie chose the broiled salmon. Benny decided he would order chicken.

As they waited for their dinners, Benny said, "We're going all the way to San Francisco."

"Quite a coincidence," said Mr. Reeves. "Quite a coincidence. I am on my way to San Francisco as well. Going to an auction. Going to seek out some very special collector's items. I have some private information that there will be some very exciting valuable things."

"What do you collect?" Henry asked.

"I collect movie memorabilia," Mr. Reeves said. He bit into a dinner roll and chewed and waved his hands as he talked. "Yes, indeed. I collect movie memorabilia."

"What exactly is movie memorabilia?" Jessie asked.

"Memorabilia, my dear young lady? Why memorabilia is a catchall phrase for all sorts of items which pertain to the movies. Early movies, mostly. Some collectors like to pick up items from modern movies and hold them indefinitely. I specialize in memorabilia from silent pictures."

"Silent pictures?" Benny asked. "What are they?"

"What *were* they," Mr. Reeves corrected. "Silent pictures were the greatest art form ever invented. Ah, yes, the silver screen has never been the same."

When Benny still looked confused, Henry explained, "Mr. Reeves is talking about the early days in the movies. At first they were just pictures on a screen and there was no sound."

"There was sound," Mr. Reeves corrected. "Music, that is. There was a piano player in the theater to add atmosphere to the movies. Have you ever even seen a silent movie on a large screen with a piano player keeping step with the action?"

When the Alden children admitted they had never seen a silent movie, Mr. Reeves shook his head sadly. "Shame. Pity, really. Too bad."

"What *exactly* do you collect?" Jessie asked.

"Memorabilia," Mr. Reeves said again, then he realized that he wasn't being clear. "I collect old movie magazines, costumes, photographs of stars, and most of all — posters. I'm on my way to San Francisco because a little bird told me there were some one-of-a-kind old movie posters coming in. Signed

Pickfords . . . that's Mary Pickford the silent movie star, and posters of movies starring Charlie Chaplin which he has autographed."

"Do they cost a lot?" Benny asked.

"The idea is to buy them from people who don't know the true value. Some autographed posters are sold for as much as fifty thousand dollars. Others go for as little as two hundred fifty dollars. Of course, autographed Pickfords and Chaplins in good condition are worth a good deal. Good night. Pleasant chatting with you." Mr. Reeves stood up abruptly and left the dining room.

"Wasn't he an unusual man?" Jessie asked.

"I liked him," Henry said.

"I really didn't understand much that he said," Benny admitted. "But I'll tell you one thing. I'd never pay fifty thousand dollars for some old poster."

"No, you wouldn't," Henry agreed, "but according to Mr. Reeves, *someone* would."

The children soon began to talk of other things. When they finished their dinner, Aunt Jane went to read, and the others told Violet all about their dinner with Mr.

Reeves. Then, they walked the entire length of the train again. As they walked, Violet said, "I wish we would run into Annie. I want to make sure she's okay."

"We could take another look in the observation lounge," Jessie offered. "That's where you talked with her last night on the other train. She may be there sketching."

They went up the stairs to the lounge and sat for a while, listening to a piano player and looking out at the stars. The sky from the observation lounge was beautiful, but they didn't see Annie. At about eight o'clock, Jessie began to yawn. She said, "I think traveling by train makes me sleepy."

Violet nodded. "It's the movement and the noise. It's a lot like being rocked in a crib and hearing someone sing a lullaby."

Benny yawned and said, "It makes me sleepy, too."

"Maybe we should go to our compartments," Violet said.

"Good idea," Benny said. "I want to see the porter make up our beds again."

"Maybe Vincent will make up the beds

and we can ask him if he's seen Annie," Violet said.

But the porter who made up their beds that night was called Tim and he didn't even know Vincent. He hadn't seen any red-haired girls named Annie, either.

That night it was Henry's turn to sleep in the top bunk. As they climbed into their beds, Henry said, "We had a big day. We saw Chicago and went to a German restaurant. We learned all about movie posters and when we wake up in the morning we'll be in Colorado."

"We will sleep all the way through Nebraska," Benny said sadly. "I wonder what Nebraska looks like?"

"Flat," Henry promised him. "That's why we can travel so far so fast. But tomorrow we'll be in the Rocky Mountains. Aunt Jane says it's some of the most beautiful scenery in the world."

"Where will we be when we wake up?" Benny asked.

"Outside of Denver. We'll have breakfast in Denver."

"But I like eating in the dining car," Benny said.

Henry laughed softly and explained. "I meant the *train* will be in Denver. *You'll* eat in the dining car."

They fell asleep very quickly. Henry was dreaming of his dog Watch when he heard a sharp knocking on the door. He called out, "Who is it?"

"It's Annie," a voice called. "Oh, please, I need your help. Please wake up!"

CHAPTER 6

The Platform Search

Benny sat up and asked, "Who is it?"

Then Henry called down from the top bunk. "Annie? Wait a minute." He jumped down as Benny slid the door open.

Annie was standing in the corridor in a bright blue robe and yellow slippers. She said, "I'm sorry to wake you, I didn't have anyone else to come to. Can you please help me?"

The door of the girls' compartment opened and Jessie asked, "What's going on?" When she saw that Henry and Benny and Annie were in the corrider, she said, "Just a minute."

In a few seconds, she and Violet were out of their compartment and also standing in the corrider. They had long sweaters over their pajamas. "What's wrong, Annie?" Violet asked.

"Please help! My portfolio was stolen and we're coming to a stop. I need you to watch the doors and make sure no one takes my portfolio off the train."

"Where are we?" Jessie asked.

Henry looked at his watch and said, "It's almost midnight. We were due to stop in Omaha, Nebraska, at midnight."

"So we get to see Nebraska after all," Benny said.

"I left my room for just a second," Annie explained, "and when I came back, the portfolio was gone! We're coming into Omaha and whoever stole my portfolio may try to take it off the train. Will you help?"

"First *you* must tell us," Jessie said. "What's *really* in that portfolio? It must be something valuable if you are so upset."

Annie nodded her head. "I'm sorry I didn't tell you the truth earlier. The portfolio is filled with my collection of old movie posters — not artwork. My aunt and I inherited them and I planned to sell them once I got to California. Now they're gone!"

"Old movie posters!" Benny cried.

"We met a man who collects old movie posters," Henry said slowly. "I wonder if Mr. Reeves knew about your collection."

"I don't think anyone knows I have the posters with me except my Aunt Ellen and my Uncle Bob," Annie said. "It was Uncle Bob who suggested I bring them to California to sell. When my aunt found out, she was furious."

"Would your aunt hire someone to steal them from you?" Jessie asked.

"Never!" Annie answered. She seemed quite upset at the question. "She would *never* do that."

Soon the children were all dressed and standing in the corridor of the sleeping car. The train began to slow down and Henry said, "We'd better spread out. Jessie, you and I are the fastest runners so we'll go as far down the train as we can. Benny, you stay here and Violet and Annie can stop halfway. Let's go before the train stops."

"What do we do if we see someone with the portfolio?" Violet asked.

"Just call for help and notice what the thief looks like," Henry said. "If we can't get help fast enough to stop him, we'll call the police and let them take care of it."

The children nodded and began running to their various stations. Henry was almost at the end of the train by the time it stopped and he stood on the steps watching carefully. Only a few people got off. They were a family with three sleeping children and several suitcases. All the suitcases were small and square, nothing that looked like a portfolio.

When the train started moving again, Henry went back toward his sleeping car and on the way he met Annie. "Did you see anyone suspicious?" she asked.

"No one," Henry admitted.

"Neither did I," Annie said. She was a

little calmer now. "I guess there's nothing more to do until morning. Thanks anyway."

"Don't you want to talk to the others?" Henry asked.

"I could see the whole platform," Annie said. "No one got off except a little old lady with a bird cage. I'm going to go back to my room now."

"Where is your room?" Henry asked.

"Up there." Annie pointed toward the second floor and down the corridor.

"Are you in this car?" Henry asked.

"No, I'm a couple of cars down," Annie answered quickly.

"What is your room number?" Henry asked.

"I've forgotten," Annie said. Then she laughed and shrugged her shoulders. "I'm sure I'll find my room, but I was so upset when I discovered the portfolio was gone, I just forgot to look at my room number."

"I'll walk you to your room," Henry offered. "But first, we need to talk to the others. Maybe they saw something suspicious."

They found the other children waiting in

the corridor. When they said they had seen nothing, Annie turned and started for the door of the sleeping car.

"Really, I'll be all right. You don't have to walk me to my room," Annie said. She turned her head, smiled, and put her hand on Henry's shoulder. "Thanks so much for your help. Now that I know the portfolio is still on the train, I can sleep."

Annie disappeared into the next car. Henry wondered what was making Annie behave so strangely. Had she seen something she didn't want to talk about? She seemed very anxious to get away from them. He decided it would be best to talk things over with the others. Henry found Jessie, Violet, and Benny waiting for him in the corridor and he suggested they go to the club car where they could talk some more.

There were only a few people still up and the four children sat in the corner and talked. "Something was funny about Annie," Henry said. "The minute the train started up again, she tried to get rid of me. Then she said she didn't remember her room number."

"That is strange," Violet agreed.

"So did anyone see anything out of the ordinary?" Henry asked.

The others shook their heads and Jessie asked, "Did you see anyone get off?"

"Just a family. Annie said she saw only an old woman." Henry shook his head. "Something doesn't make sense."

"We saw something funny *on* the train," Benny said.

"Yes," Jessie added. "When we were coming back, we saw Vincent talking with that man with the beard and sunglasses — the man we had dinner with on the first train. They talked for a long time."

"Why was he wearing sunglasses in the middle of the night?" Violet asked.

"I think he was wearing a disguise," Benny said. "My detective kit comes with a beard and sunglasses. Maybe he has a kit just like it."

"Maybe Annie's wrong," Henry said. "Maybe Annie's aunt did hire someone to steal the posters."

"Maybe she hired Vincent to take the

posters," Jessie said. "We did see Annie's aunt give him money."

"But Annie is certain her aunt wouldn't hire anyone to do anything like that," Violet said. "I think she knows her aunt well."

Henry shook his head. "We still don't know much."

Then Benny yawned and stretched. He said, "I'm sleepy."

"We should go back to sleep," Jessie said. "We don't want to be tired tomorrow."

"Tomorrow we'll see the Rocky Mountains," Henry said. Then he added, "Tomorrow we can talk about Annie's problem at breakfast."

"That's a good idea," Benny said. "I am a better thinker when I am wide-awake."

The Alden children were back in bed and fast asleep in ten minutes.

CHAPTER 7

Shadowing Vincent

When the Boxcar Children woke up the train was slowing down and Aunt Jane was knocking on their door. "We're almost in Denver," she called. "Time to get up."

They were dressed in just a few minutes. "Why don't we have breakfast in the station," Henry suggested. He wanted to make sure no one got off the train with Annie's portfolio.

Aunt Jane said that would be fine and so the Aldens got off the train and went into the

Denver station. They watched the train exits at the same time they bought postcards and ate cinnamon rolls, orange juice, and milk.

After breakfast, they walked around a little bit. They all agreed it felt funny to be on solid ground again.

"That's what sailors used to call getting sea legs," Henry said. "Even after you get off the train you feel as though you're still on it. It's the same on a boat."

"See, I told you riding a train is a lot like sailing," Benny said. "I guess it's because you need sea legs for both."

"Look over there." Violet pointed to a magazine stand.

"That's Mr. Reeves," Jessie said. "I wonder why he got off the train? I thought he was going to San Francisco."

"Maybe he wanted to stretch his legs like us," Benny said.

"Maybe," Jessie said. "But let's watch him carefully. It's very odd that he collects movie posters, and Annie's movie posters were stolen."

"No portfolio in sight," Henry said. "He's

just buying a newspaper." The children watched as Mr. Reeves put the newspaper under his arm and headed back for the train.

They hurried to catch up with him. "There you are," Mr. Reeves said, as though he had been looking for them. "I was wondering what happened to you nice young people and your lovely aunt. Perhaps we can have lunch together? Of course, we can't all lunch at one table. But we could sit side by side and pass the rolls or something. Right?"

"That would be nice," Henry said.

"Good," Mr. Reeves said. "How about lunch today? No — I'm busy today. Tomorrow at noon? Is it a date?"

As Mr. Reeves went on his way, Jessie whispered to Henry, "He sure looks cheerful. Do you think it's possible . . . ?"

"I can't believe he's a thief," Benny said. "I like Mr. Reeves."

"He was awfully happy. Maybe it's because he got what he wanted," Henry said. "Let's wait as long as we can before we get back on the train and make sure no one comes off carrying a portfolio."

Mr. Reeves went back into the train with his newspaper tucked under his arm. The Aldens watched carefully as a few more passengers got off and others got on the train. No one saw anything out of the ordinary.

Henry said, "I wish we could help Annie find her portfolio."

"I just hope we can find *Annie*," Violet said softly. "I'd like to talk with her again."

"Where do you think she might be?" Jessie asked.

"Let's go to our compartment and go over the clues," Henry said. "Then we can decide what to do."

Aunt Jane was surprised when the children said they were going back to their compartment. "I thought you would want to ride in the observation car all day. We could have snacks instead of lunch and then have a really nice dinner to celebrate crossing the Continental Divide."

"What's the Continental Divide?" Benny asked.

"It's a high ridge of mountains that divides the United States," Henry explained. "All the rivers on the east side of the Continental Divide flow into the Mississippi River. All the rivers on the west side of the Continental Divide run into the Colorado River or the Pacific Ocean."

"This train is tilting up," Violet said. "Are we going up the mountains now?"

"We're beginning our steep climb," Aunt Jane said. "It's very steep for the next two hours. I think you'd see more in the observation car."

"We'll be up there soon," Henry promised. "We just need to talk something over. You go on up and we'll meet you."

The Alden children went into the girls' compartment and sat down to think. Henry started the conversation by saying, "I think we need to go over our questions and clues. We can't help Annie unless we know what is going on."

"The man with the beard and sunglasses is a clue," Benny said promptly.

"Why do you think that?" Henry asked.

"I don't know," Benny said. "I just have

a feeling he's connected to Annie. Also, who is he? Why was he talking so long to Vincent?"

"The money Annie's aunt gave Vincent is a clue," said Jessie. "It was a lot of money for a tip. Why would her aunt pay Vincent to look after Annie if she was angry?"

"She *was* angry," Violet said. "Do you think she really paid Vincent to steal the posters?"

"Maybe Vincent is working with the bearded man to steal Annie's portfolio," Benny suggested.

"We don't *really* know what was in Annie's portfolio," Henry said. "We didn't see the movie posters. And we do know Annie doesn't always tell the truth."

"I think Annie was telling the truth about the posters," Violet said quietly.

"How do you know?" Jessie asked.

Violet began, "I notice things. When people don't tell the truth, they don't like to look at you. Annie looked right at me when she talked about going to live with her uncle and selling her posters."

"But she wouldn't look at me last night, after we helped her look for anyone who was getting off the train with her portfolio," Henry said. "Plus, she definitely did not want to tell me where her room was. She was hiding something last night."

"That's another clue," Benny said. Then he asked, "What about Mr. Reeves? Don't you think it's strange he's on the same train as Annie? He collects old movie posters and he says he's going to San Francisco to buy some. But what if he really planned to steal them from Annie?"

"Yes, Mr. Reeves is definitely a suspect," Jessie agreed.

"So we have Annie, the bearded man with the sunglasses, Vincent, and Mr. Reeves," Jessie said. "Any one of them could be the thief."

"Not Annie," Violet said. "The posters are hers."

"We don't know that for sure," Henry reminded his sister. "How do we know they're really hers? Maybe she stole them from her aunt."

Violet frowned because she didn't like that idea. She said, "Annie is a nice person and I believe she was telling the truth about the posters."

"It sounds like we have some good ideas," Henry said, "but we don't know where any of these people are. Let's go up to the observation lounge and see the Rocky Mountains. Sooner or later one of our suspects will show up to see the scenery."

"The observation lounge sounds like a good place to start," Violet said. "I'll take my sketch pad."

The Aldens went up to the observation car where Aunt Jane waited for them. She said, "I'm so happy you're here. This is the most fabulous scenery I've ever seen. But there aren't any more chairs, I'm afraid."

"That's okay," Jessie said.

The children settled down on the floor close to their aunt. They gazed out the window as the train twisted through narrow canyons and around the high mountain peaks. They had spectacular views of the beautiful Rocky Mountains.

Vincent came to the observation lounge and stopped in the entrance. He looked up and down the car and when he saw the Aldens he turned away.

Henry stood up. "I think I'll see where he is going. I'll be back soon."

Henry followed Vincent from a distance, making sure that the porter didn't notice him. He watched as Vincent went up and down the aisles of the coach cars, bringing pillows and blankets to people who wanted them. After about ten minutes, Vincent knocked on the door of a sleeping compartment. The door opened and Vincent went in.

Henry stood outside the door, trying to hear what Vincent was saying. All he could make out was that the porter was talking to a man. Then the door started to open again. Vincent stepped out into the hallway.

Henry was bending down, pretending to tie his sneaker. He heard Vincent say, "Then it's settled. You'll be leaving the train at Salt Lake City?"

"It's settled," the man said in a gruff voice.

Henry followed Vincent into the kitchen

where he saw the porter sit down at a table. He had a cup of coffee and a newspaper in front of him.

Henry went back and knocked on the door of the sleeping compartment, where he had seen Vincent before. The door opened a bit and someone said, "Yes?"

"Is Billy there?" Henry asked, making up a name. The door was open just a crack and Henry could see only a part of the man's face, but he recognized the sunglasses and beard.

"No. I don't know any Billy." The man shut the door in Henry's face.

Henry went quickly back to the observation lounge and sat down on the floor beside the others. Violet looked up from her sketching and asked Henry, "Any news?"

"I followed Vincent and he talked to the bearded man. He's getting off at Salt Lake City tonight."

"I really wish we could find Annie's room," Violet said. "I'm worried about her."

Aunt Jane left her card game and came over to the children. She said, "Good, you are all here. We are going through Moffat

Tunnel now. This is the way we cross the Continental Divide."

The tunnel seemed very long and the children were glad they were all together. The train wasn't dark but it was very dark outside. Most of the people in the observation lounge sat quietly and looked out at the black walls of the tunnel without saying anything.

When they came out into the daylight, Violet looked up and smiled. "There's Annie," she said. She called over to Annie and said, "Come join us."

Annie waved to Violet and started toward them. She was limping and as she sat down on the floor beside Henry, she winced with pain. She bent over to stroke her ankle and said, "It's good to see you all. I didn't thank you for helping me last night."

"Why are you limping?" Violet asked.

"I sprained my ankle this morning," Annie said. "I thought I saw someone with a package that looked like my portfolio leaving the train in Denver and I jumped off to try and catch up with him. I fell and sprained my ankle."

"Did you catch the person?" Violet asked.

"No." Annie frowned. Then she said, "It will be all right, though. I'm not worried about the portfolio anymore because the insurance company will cover the loss."

"We watched people get off in Denver," Henry said. "It's funny we didn't see you fall."

Annie ignored Henry's comment and asked, "Isn't this a fabulous trip?"

"I wish I had seen your posters," Benny said. "I'd like to see movie posters which are worth so much money."

Annie said, "The posters are gone — that's all there is to it. So let's not talk about sad things. I think we're about to go down the mountain."

Annie sat with them for a little while. Her ankle obviously hurt her a lot but she said she was all right. "The conductor helped me bandage my ankle," she said. "I'll be all right."

Annie watched Violet sketch interesting people in the observation lounge. About five o'clock, the bearded man with the sunglasses came in for a drink and Violet made a quick sketch of him while he stood at the drinks counter. He took his drink with him and left the car quickly.

Violet showed the sketch to Annie and asked, "Doesn't he have unusual ears? They are flat on the side but a little pointed on top."

"Yes, his ears are certainly different." Annie studied it carefully and said, "You know, there's something familiar about that man."

"Do you know him?" Henry asked.

Annie looked carefully at the sketch and shook her head. "No. I've never seen him before in my life."

"Are you sure?" Henry asked.

Annie looked at him with a steady gaze. "I've never seen him before in my life," she repeated quietly. "Why do you ask?"

Henry answered, "Annie, we want to be your friends but we aren't certain you've told us everything."

"Of course I have," Annie answered quickly. But this time she flushed and looked away.

CHAPTER 8

Good Friends

Aunt Jane suggested that Annie join them for dinner that night. "That way we can split up without having one person sit alone," she said. "We'd love to have you."

"Oh, do," Violet urged. "We can sit together."

Annie smiled at Violet and said, "I'd love to. I'll meet you at six but I think I should go back to my room now."

The Aldens were waiting when Annie limped into the dining room at quarter past six. She was still wearing the same jeans and sweater and her face looked flushed. She said, "I fell asleep. I'm sorry."

"That's all right," Aunt Jane said. "I'm sure you're in a lot of pain."

They found three tables with two people and so they split into three groups. Benny and Henry joined one table, and Jessie and Aunt Jane joined the second. Violet and Annie sat together at the third table.

Violet was pleased to have a chance to talk with her new friend. They talked most of the time about sketching but Violet learned quite a bit more about her. By the time dinner was finished, Violet learned that Annie was eighteen years old and an only child. She also learned that seven was her lucky number. Annie said, "I was really happy when I saw my room number — seven hundred seventy-seven. I thought maybe it would bring me some luck — I guess it didn't."

"Five is my lucky number," Violet said. "I'm glad you can remember your room number now."

Annie looked away and quickly changed

the subject. "Purple is my favorite color."

"That's my favorite color, too," Violet said.

"I noticed," Annie said. "Do you wear only purple clothes?"

"I have some others," Violet said, "but I thought it would be easier for this trip if they were all one color. That left more room for my art supplies."

The waiter brought the bill and Annie said, "Oh, dear, I left my purse in my room. Will you wait here for me? I'll go get it and be right back."

"Did you lock yourself out? Are your keys in your purse?" Violet asked.

Annie frowned. "I must have left my door unlocked. I was so sleepy and my ankle hurts so much that I'm not thinking very well."

Violet stood up. "I'll go get your purse. I can tell your ankle still hurts a lot."

"No, don't!" Annie called.

But Violet was already on her way.

Violet found Room 777 easily. It was on the second floor of the sleeping car behind the dining car. She peeked in the room and saw Annie's purse on the sofa. And there on the chair was Annie's large, black portfolio.

Violet picked up the purse and closed the door carefully. She was back in the dining room in just a few seconds. Annie was waiting for her.

"Annie, when I was in your room, I saw . . ."

"I know," Annie said. "You saw the portfolio."

"Why did you lie?" Violet asked quietly.

Annie leaned over and touched Violet's arm. "Oh, please let me explain." She looked over at Jessie, Henry, and Benny and said, "I'd like them to hear, too."

The other Aldens joined their table and Annie began to talk.

"In a way," Annie said, "I was angry because my aunt wanted me to give her half the money for the poster sale. She doesn't need the money and I do, so I thought I'd say they were stolen. Then, when it was safe, I'd sell the poster collection and keep all the money. I thought if I asked you to help me I would have witnesses to prove they were stolen.

"So no one was after the posters at all?" Jessie said.

"No. I made it all up." As she talked, tears streamed down her face.

"What?" said Henry. "But you woke us up in the night and told us it was stolen!"

Then Annie said, "I know, I'm very sorry. I'm glad you know the truth. Now I can't go through with my plan and I won't have to feel so guilty. You have all been so nice to me and I haven't been honest with you. I'm so sorry."

"We knew you weren't telling the whole truth," Violet said. "You're not very good at making up stories."

"I know." Annie choked back her tears and smiled. "I blush and I get mixed up. You see, I don't usually lie about things. I really am an honest person. Or at least, I used to be . . ." She began to cry again.

Jessie handed her a Kleenex and Annie blew her nose. Then she said, "I'm really glad you found out. Now I'm glad, too, that I can't go through with the scheme. My aunt always loved me and took care of me as best she could."

Annie began to cry again. "When we quarreled she fell down. I don't even know if she's hurt. I just ran away."

"She's all right," Henry said. "I helped her up. How did you hurt your ankle?"

"I sprained it trying to hide the portfolio on the top bunk. I thought I could do it but I couldn't. And then I fell down." Then Annie said, "I'm so sorry."

Then Violet said to her brother, "We should help Annie to her room. Her ankle hurts a lot and she's very tired."

Henry nodded and helped Annie up. He said, "Lean on me."

"Her room is number seven hundred seventy-seven," Violet said.

Annie looked at Violet and smiled. "Thank you, Violet. You're a good friend."

The Aldens helped Annie down the hallway and up the stairs to her compartment. When they got to her room, Annie said,

"You might as well come in and see the posters."

"I'd like to," Benny said. "I want to see a Pickford."

Annie smiled. "How did you know? I have two signed posters of Mary Pickford's first movie. They are worth a great deal of money. And I have four signed posters of Charlie Chaplin."

Henry and Jessie looked at each other. They were both wondering why Annie just happened to have the kinds of posters that Mr. Reeves hoped to add to his collection.

Annie led them into her compartment. She unzipped the portfolio and opened it. She stared down at the portfolio and then looked at the Aldens in amazement. Finally, she said, "It's empty!"

"Yes," Jessie agreed. "It's empty."

"But what can that mean?" Annie asked. "How can that be?"

"Is there something else you want to tell us?" Violet asked Annie gently.

"No! Honestly, I know it must be hard to

believe me because I've told so many stories. But I don't know what happened to the posters. It's like a bad dream coming true. Where could they have gone?"

"Someone must have known you had the posters," Henry said. "That person waited until you left your room and then took the posters out."

"Without the portfolio," Jessie noted. "That means they'll be easier to hide."

"If the posters are folded and damaged, they'll lose most of their value," Annie said. "I can't believe this is happening. Maybe someone wanted to see them and borrowed them for a while."

"I'm afraid the posters were really stolen this time," Jessie said.

"Really stolen!" Annie began to laugh and then she began to cry again. She slumped into one of the chairs and asked, "What will I do? I don't have anything without the posters. I won't be able to pay for my room and board. I won't be able to go to art school."

"I thought you said you had insurance?" Violet asked.

Annie shook her head. "I made that up, too. There is no insurance." She sobbed until Violet thought Annie's heart would break.

It was Benny who patted Annie on the arm and said, "Don't worry, Annie. We will find your posters for you."

CHAPTER 9

Recovered Property

The Aldens called a porter and got him to make up Annie's room early so she could rest. "Stay here," Violet said. "Your ankle hurts you and you're very upset. Rest will do you good."

"But what if the person who has my posters gets off the train while I'm sleeping?" Annie asked.

"You really can't move fast enough to be much help," Jessie pointed out. "We can, though. We'll watch for you."

"Leave it to us," Benny said. "We'll catch the thief very soon."

Annie smiled at him and Violet realized her friend was feeling better.

"We'll watch very carefully. If anyone gets off with a large package, we'll call for help," Henry said.

"What time does the train stop again?" Annie asked. Her voice already sounded sleepy.

"I have my timetable," Henry said. "It stops in Salt Lake City at eleven-thirty-six p.m."

"You won't be able to stay awake that late," Annie protested.

"We'll wake up and then go back to sleep. Just like we did when you called us to help you last night," Violet said.

Annie made a face. "I used an alarm clock. Anyway, that was very wrong of me."

"We'd like to borrow your alarm clock," Henry said. "You can sleep through till morning."

Annie nodded and smiled. "You are very grown-up children. I feel like the youngest one here tonight."

"We learned to take care of ourselves when we lived in our boxcar," Violet explained. "Before our Grandfather found us and took us to live in Greenfield, we did everything for ourselves."

The children went to bed early and Jessie set the alarm clock for eleven o'clock. "That will give us time to get up and dressed so we can watch the platform when we stop in Salt Lake City at eleven-thirty-six," Jessie said.

The alarm went off at exactly eleven o'clock. Jessie and Violet woke up easily and knocked on the door of the boys' room. They all pulled their clothes over their pajamas and got ready to station themselves by the doors of the train for the second night in a row.

"At least tonight we know a little bit more than we did," Henry said. "I knew Annie wasn't being quite truthful but I didn't know she'd staged the whole thing."

"You believe her now, don't you?" Violet asked.

"Yes, I do," Henry said. "Someone really

stole the posters this time. I'm just not sure who that someone could be."

"It could be Mr. Reeves," Jessie said. "He is certainly interested in posters."

"It could be Vincent," Violet said. "He took money from Annie's aunt and he . . ."

"It could be that guy with the sunglasses and the beard," Benny said. "He was talking to Vincent . . ."

"It could be someone we don't know at all," Henry said. "But whoever it is would have a big package. Annie says folding the posters would lower their worth."

"So we'll keep a sharp eye out for large packages," Jessie said.

The children nodded and stood waiting until the train pulled to a full halt.

They leaned out the door and looked up and down the platform. There were too many people moving around to be sure of seeing everything. "We'll have to get out," Henry said.

They jumped off the train and began moving up and down the platform, looking from one group of people to another. Suddenly, Jessie called, "I see the bearded man!"

"And he's holding a big rolled package," Violet said.

"Vincent is helping him," Benny shouted. He began to run. At that moment, Vincent turned and went back into the train. The bearded man walked quickly away.

"Hurry, let's catch him." Jessie darted forward and caught hold of the man's coat sleeve. She said, "Wait a minute, please. We want to talk to you."

"Go away," the man said.

Benny grabbed the back of his coat and Henry and Jessie tried to get hold of the rolled package.

The bearded man looked around at the crowd that was beginning to gather. He jerked the package away from the Alden children and threw it on the platform. Henry, Jessie, and Violet all ran for the package. Only Benny held onto the coattail and as the man pulled away from him, Benny was left holding a piece of the coat.

When the others came back with the package, Benny said, "He got away."

"Never mind," Jessie said. She bent down and untied the string around the rolled package. Unwrapping the paper carefully, she let the posters fall flat. "The important thing is we've got Annie's posters back."

"But the bearded man got away and we don't know who he was or how he even knew the posters were on the train," Benny said regretfully.

"Where is Vincent?" Jessie asked.

"He went back on the train," Henry said. "I am not even sure he saw us."

"We can talk about it in the morning," Violet said. "Let's get back to bed now before Aunt Jane misses us."

But when they got back to their compartment, Aunt Jane was sitting up on the side of her bed waiting for them. She asked, "Where have you been? I was beginning to worry."

"We caught the man who stole some posters," Benny said. Then he corrected himself. "We caught the posters but the man got away."

"What happened?" Aunt Jane asked.

"Annie has some valuable movie posters," Violet answered. "She said they were stolen and they weren't. Then later they *were* stolen and now we've recovered them."

Aunt Jane smiled and said, "It sounds complicated. Maybe you can explain in the morning."

"Tomorrow morning, we'll tell you the whole story. It *is* complicated," Henry said.

The next morning, the Alden children told Aunt Jane all about their adventures with Annie and the posters. When Henry got to the part about following Vincent, she nodded. "I knew something was going on but I thought it was some sort of a game you were playing."

"No, it wasn't a game," Henry explained. Then he added, "But I still want to talk to Vincent. I think it is odd he talked so often to the bearded man. Maybe he knows more than he is telling."

"I want to talk to Annie," Aunt Jane said.

"Do you think we should wake her and tell her we've recovered the posters?" Violet asked.

"Let her sleep as long as she can," Aunt Jane said. "Her ankle will heal faster if she is resting."

They agreed that Annie would be very happy to have her posters back. Then Jessie said, "But there is still so much we don't know."

"Yes," Violet said. "How could the bearded man know that she had the posters? Do you think Annie's aunt could have anything to do with it?"

"It doesn't seem like that could happen," Jessie said. "On the other hand, how did Mr. Reeves know about the old posters coming into San Francisco?"

"We can probably find out more when Annie wakes up," Benny said.

CHAPTER 10

Meeting Uncle Bob

Annie found them in the observation lounge when she woke up. Benny said, "I told you we'd get your posters back!"

The Aldens told her all about the bearded man and recovering the posters. Annie listened carefully and then she shook her head. "I still don't know how he knew what I had in my portfolio."

"Someone must have told him," Henry said. "Maybe you told a friend and you've forgotten."

Annie shook her head. "I didn't tell anyone."

"Aunt Jane would like to talk to you," Jessie said. "She asked us to let her know when you were up."

Annie looked a little frightened as she stood up.

"I'll go get her," Benny said. "She doesn't want you to walk on that ankle."

Very soon, Aunt Jane and Benny came back. Annie and Aunt Jane went to a small table in a corner to talk. The Aldens sat a long way from them. They talked about their trip and about their adventure in Salt Lake City. From time to time, one of them glanced over at the table where Aunt Jane and Annie sat alone.

Jessie said, "Annie looks pretty upset and she isn't saying much."

"I hope they don't quarrel," Violet said. "I want Annie to be my friend for always."

"We'll just have to wait and see," Jessie said. "Where are we?"

"We're in Nevada," Henry answered. "We're on our way to Reno."

"Nevada is beautiful," Violet answered. "Look over there at those purple hills. And see those mountains in the distance? They are all reds and purples and blues."

"I'll be glad to see San Francisco," Benny said. "But I wish the train ride was even longer."

"Three nights and three days went fast, didn't they?" Jessie said.

"The day is early," Henry said. "We're still in Nevada and we have a whole day of California coming up."

The children looked out the window at the beautiful landscape and hoped that Aunt Jane and Annie would be finished talking soon. Then Annie stood up and walked out of the dining room.

Finally, Violet could stand no more suspense. She went to Aunt Jane's table and asked, "Where's Annie?"

Aunt Jane smiled. "She's gone to rest. She's decided to telephone her aunt at the next stop. She doesn't want to wait until we get to San Francisco to make her apology. She is also going to see if she can find out who her aunt talked to about her trip. We just can't understand how anyone knew she would be on the train with her posters."

The other Alden children came over to Aunt Jane's table and she said, "Annie is very grateful for your help. And I want you to know how proud I am of you. You are very kind and brave children — and smart, too. I'm proud of my nieces and nephews."

"I still want to know who that man with the beard is," Benny said. "The mystery won't be solved until we figure that out."

"Don't forget about Vincent and Mr. Reeves," Jessie said.

Annie came back to the dining room. She was smiling and she seemed quite happy. "I had a nice talk with my aunt and she's not angry anymore. But she says she didn't tell anyone I was taking this trip. She says she kept thinking I would change my mind. I don't understand how, but that bearded man must have learned about the posters some other way." Annie shrugged. "The important thing is that I have the posters back.

Thanks to you." She hugged each of the Boxcar Children.

"Are we going to sit in the dining room until lunch?" Aunt Jane teased. "Don't you want to go up to the observation lounge this morning? Most people think this is the best scenery of our trip."

"The Sierra Nevadas," Benny said proudly. "Mile-high mountains."

"Let's go," Violet said. "I want to see everything I can on this trip."

They left the dining car and went to the observation lounge. Aunt Jane found a group of bridge players and joined their game. The Aldens sat watching the Sierra Nevada mountains roll by their window. Violet tried to sketch the tall pine trees but soon gave up. "I'll have to learn to draw faster before I can sketch landscapes from a train window."

"You can use my photographs when we get home," Jessie offered. "With my snapshots and your memory, I'm sure you'll do fine."

They enjoyed the scenery so much that they stopped talking about the bearded man and the posters until Vincent came into the observation lounge.

"There's Vincent," said Benny. "He's a suspect — we should talk to him. He was helping the bearded man."

But Vincent went right over to the Alden children, asking, "Are you having a good time?"

"Wonderful," Jessie replied. "We're sorry this is the last day."

Vincent nodded and looked down at Violet's sketchbook. He asked, "Mind if I look at your drawings?"

Violet gave him the sketchbook and he turned the pages slowly, saying, "You're a good artist, young lady."

He stopped and looked a long time at the sketch of the bearded man. "Do you know that man?" Henry asked.

"Funny guy," Vincent answered. "Had a ticket to San Francisco but he got off in Salt Lake City."

"Is he a friend of yours?" Jessie asked.

Vincent closed the sketchbook and handed

it back to Violet. "No, just a guy on a train. I helped him with his luggage, that's all. He gave me a good tip."

"You helped him carry a rolled package," Benny said. "The package had stolen posters in it."

"How do you know that?" Vincent asked. He was smiling as though he thought they were joking. "Were they your posters?"

"These were very valuable posters," Henry added. "They weren't ours, they belonged to our friend, Annie."

"Annie," Vincent said. "She's the one I was supposed to watch over." Then Vincent's face fell. "I guess I didn't do a very good job. If she really lost the posters she needs to report it to the railroad police."

Vincent left them then and the Alden children talked it over. "He certainly seemed to be telling the truth," Jessie said.

"But you never know," Benny added. "Sometimes things look one way and they turn out another way."

"He looked a long time at my sketch of the

bearded man," Violet pointed out.

"What do you think we should do next?" Jessie asked.

"If Vincent is telling the truth and Annie's aunt says no one knew about the posters, there isn't much to go on," Henry said.

"Let's talk to Mr. Reeves," Jessie suggested. "He seems to be rushing to buy exactly the kind of old movie posters that Annie wants to sell. It seems like more than a coincidence."

Henry looked at his watch. "We are having lunch with Mr. Reeves in an hour. Maybe we will learn something then."

"I think I'll go visit Annie," Violet said. "She must be lonely in her compartment."

"Maybe she will have lunch with us," Jessie suggested.

"I'm sure she'd like that," Violet answered. "She and Benny and I can sit together and you and Henry can sit with Aunt Jane and Mr. Reeves."

At lunchtime, Mr. Reeves was waiting for

Aunt Jane and Jessie and Henry. He was in a very good mood and he talked and talked about his life and his interests. As lunch was served, Henry asked, "Do you mind if I ask how you found out about the posters you are planning to buy?"

Mr. Reeves smiled and said, "Collectors like to keep their sources confidential. Are you planning to snatch them out from under my nose?" Then he looked suspiciously at Henry and asked, "Why do you want to know?"

"We're just curious," Jessie answered promptly.

"I'm curious why you would be curious," Mr. Reeves said and then he laughed at his own joke. He looked straight at Henry and asked directly, "Why *do* you want to know?"

"It's kind of a mystery," Henry said. "A friend has some posters and we're trying to help her."

"A mystery?" Mr. Reeves said. "Delightful. I love a mystery. Many of my favorite movie posters are about mysteries."

"So how did you hear about the posters you are going to San Francisco to buy?" Jessie prompted.

"A collector never tells his sources," Mr. Reeves said. "Especially if you have a friend in the business."

"She's not actually in the business," Henry said. He looked at Jessie and Aunt Jane and they both nodded that he should go on and tell the story. "We met a young woman on this train and she has some valuable posters. Someone tried to rob her." He cleared his voice and said, "The fact is, the posters sound like the same ones you were describing. She has signed posters of Mary Pickford and Charlie Chaplin and some other silent screen stars."

"And she's here!" Mr. Reeves said with excitement. "I must speak to her immediately."

"We want to know how you knew those kinds of posters would be for sale in San Francisco," Henry said.

"Very well, a man named Perkins called me and said he'd have the posters for sale on

Friday. I don't fly so I popped onto this train so I could be there by Friday. You say the girl has the posters with her? I suppose she's the redhead sitting with your brother and sister." Mr. Reeves stood up and went toward the table where Annie, Violet, and Benny were sitting. Henry and Jessie followed.

They reached Annie's table just as Mr. Reeves was introducing himself. He gave Annie his card, bowed to her, and then asked, "I understand you have some posters to sell. I wonder if they really are the ones I'm traveling out to see."

"I don't think they could be," Annie said. "No one knew I was bringing them out to California except my aunt."

"A man called Perkins called me," Mr. Reeves said. "I've done business with a friend of his before."

"Bob Perkins?" Annie asked. She seemed very surprised.

"Yes, do you know him?"

"He's my uncle. I don't actually know him," Annie admitted. "But I've talked to him on the telephone and he knew I was bringing the posters . . . I forgot that . . . but why?" Annie's voice trailed off and she said, "I wonder why he called you without telling me about it."

"I'm a fairly well-known collector," Mr. Reeves said. "It's natural that he might call me. May I see the posters now? Perhaps we can strike a bargain before the train gets into San Francisco."

Annie shook her head. "I'm not selling."

"But, my dear, I've come all the way from Chicago!"

"I'm sorry," Annie said. "I talked it over with my aunt and we decided I shouldn't sell." To the Aldens, she added, "My aunt says she'll send me an allowance if I really want to live with Uncle Bob."

"I would make you a very fair offer," Mr. Reeves said. "A very *fine* offer if the posters are in the condition your uncle promised."

"I'm sorry," Annie said firmly.

"Your uncle did promise to sell them to me, you know." Mr. Reeves seemed quite disappointed.

"They weren't his to sell," Annie said simply. "The posters are an inheritance from my grandparents and they were left to me and my aunt. It is our decision."

"I see." Mr. Reeves bowed and said, "Well, children. Let us go back to our table and have lunch before it gets too cold."

When they rejoined Aunt Jane, Mr. Reeves said, "This is a nuisance but I shall just have to turn around and go back to Chicago. She has no intention of selling the posters. Her uncle was mistaken."

"So it was her uncle who called you," Aunt Jane said quietly. "I wonder why."

"It seems he had no right to offer the posters for sale," Mr. Reeves said. "Ah, well, perhaps the trip across the country has been good for my nerves."

He stood up abruptly and bowed. "It's been a pleasure. You are fine children. Goodbye to you all."

Mr. Reeves turned to leave the dining car. Henry stood up and said, "I think I'll follow him, just to be safe."

"I'll go with you," Jessie said.

They followed Mr. Reeves to his room and then went up to Annie's room to wait for her. When she arrived, Henry asked, "Will you check on your posters just to make sure they're safe?"

Annie went into her compartment and in a few minutes she came out smiling. "Everything is fine. Thanks a lot."

"We're going back to the observation lounge," Jessie said. "Do you want to come along?"

"No. I think I'll feel safer if I sit right here," Annie said. "Besides, my ankle is still a little weak. I'll just sit here and think."

"Why do you think your uncle called Mr. Reeves to sell your posters?" Jessie asked.

Annie shook her head and looked troubled. "I really don't know Uncle Bob. My aunt never talks about him but it's clear she doesn't like him. When I began to quarrel with her, I wrote to him. He telephoned me a few times and then he said he really wanted me to come out to California to live. He was the one who suggested I could sell the posters to pay for my education."

"So you've never even seen him?" Henry asked.

She said, "He's coming to meet me in Emeryville where the train stops and we'll take the bus into San Francisco. He said he'll be wearing a red tie."

"We'll help you find him," Jessie promised.

"Thanks," Annie said. "You've been good friends. See you at five."

At exactly five p.m. the train pulled into the station in Oakland, California. There was a bus waiting to take all the passengers who were going to downtown San Francisco.

Annie said, "Won't you wait and meet my uncle?"

"That would be very nice," Aunt Jane said. "We'd like to invite you to visit us while the children are here."

"There's a man over there in a green jacket and a red tie," Benny said. He pointed to a dark-haired slender man.

Annie and the others went over to the man. She said, "Uncle Bob?"

"Annie? Is that you? I'm so glad to see

you." Her uncle put his arms around her and hugged her.

Violet looked very upset and she said to Henry, "I know that man. He was on the train with us. He's the one with the beard and sunglasses."

"How would you know that?" Henry asked.

"I recognize his ears," Violet said. "I'm certain I'm right."

When Henry looked doubtful, Violet called out to Annie, "Come here, please, I have something to say."

Annie stepped away from her Uncle Bob and came over to Violet and Henry.

Violet said, "Annie, he's the one who tried to steal your posters. He had on a fake beard and sunglasses but I'm certain it's him. Here, let me show you."

Violet dropped her suitcase onto the ground and knelt beside it. She opened up the suitcase and pulled out her sketch pad. She began to flip through the pages as she said, "You're an artist, Annie. You'll see what I mean. Look at his ears. Now look at the ears on this man in the sketch. They are the same, aren't they?"

Annie looked at the sketch. Then she looked at her uncle. Then she looked at the sketch and then she turned kind of white and asked, "Are you really my Uncle Bob?"

"Of course I am." The man laughed and pulled out his driver's license with a picture on it. "I guess it's right to be cautious. After all, you've never met me even though you are my only niece. I'll carry the posters." He tried to take the portfolio from Henry but Henry held on tight.

"I met a man on the train who said you'd promised to sell him my posters," Annie said. "That wasn't your decision to make, Uncle Bob."

"Don't be silly," her uncle said. "I was just trying to help. Here, son, I'll take those posters." He tugged and Henry held on tighter.

Annie took a deep breath and said, "I don't think so. You tried to steal my posters on the train. You were wearing sunglasses and a beard but you were the same size and coloring. And I have a drawing of your ears."

Uncle Bob pretended to laugh. "That's ridiculous," he said. "How could I be on a train with you and then meet you here? You kids are making up crazy stories."

"No, sir," Henry said. "I think it's quite simple. You got off the train in Salt Lake City. We chased you and Benny tore a piece out of your coat."

"I think you might remember that if you try," Jessie added.

"Annie, I don't know who these people are but you should come home with me. I'm your uncle."

"These people are my friends," Annie said decisively. "They will help me get to the airport and I'll fly home to Aunt Ellen tonight. I was a silly girl to think I was ready to make it on my own."

"All right," Uncle Bob said. "You go, but leave the posters with me. That old lady has plenty of other money and these should have been mine."

He made a grab for the posters but Henry

was too fast for him. He jerked the portfolio away from Uncle Bob.

"I still say the posters are mine," he shouted. "They belonged to my parents."

"We have a will," Annie reminded him.

"That will is unfair," he said. "My parents were unfair! They never should have cut me out! It isn't fair!"

"I'm sorry for you, Uncle Bob. You must be very unhappy. But I can't stay here."

"If we don't hurry, we'll all be staying here," Benny said. He pointed to the bus and said, "Our bus is leaving. We'd better go, too."

The Alden children, Aunt Jane, and Annie all picked up their suitcases and ran for the bus. They were the last ones on board but there were plenty of seats so they were able to sit together.

Aunt Jane smiled at Annie and said, "You showed very good sense, Annie."

"It was Violet who had good sense," Annie said.

"You were quick to see that he was the

same man," Henry said to his little sister. "That was good work."

Violet smiled and said, "We all helped." Then she said to Annie, "I'm glad you're coming with us. You can meet our Uncle Andy."

Aunt Jane said, "We'll call your Aunt Ellen when we get home and see if you can spend a few days sightseeing with us. Then you can go home to Boston. I know your aunt will be glad to see you."

"Yes," Annie agreed. "And I will be glad to see her."

"And I'll be glad because you will be living in Boston again," Violet said. "We live in Greenfield and that isn't far away at all."

"We can be good friends," Annie said and hugged her.

"And I'm glad because we solved the mystery of the long train ride," said Benny. "It was a very good mystery, too. I was surprised right up until the very end."

"So were we all," Violet said as she squeezed into the seat beside him.

GERTRUDE CHANDLER WARNER discovered when she was teaching that many readers who like an exciting story could find no books that were both easy and fun to read. She decided to try to meet this need, and her first book, *The Boxcar Children*, quickly proved she had succeeded.

Miss Warner drew on her own experiences to write the mystery. As a child she spent hours watching trains go by on the tracks opposite her family home. She often dreamed about what it would be like to set up housekeeping in a caboose or freight car — the situation the Alden children find themselves in.

When Miss Warner received requests for more adventures involving Henry, Jessie, Violet, and Benny Alden, she began additional stories. In each, she chose a special setting and introduced unusual or eccentric characters who liked the unpredictable.

While the mystery element is central to each of Miss Warner's books, she never thought of them as strictly juvenile mysteries. She liked to stress the Aldens' independence and resourcefulness and their solid New England devotion to using up and making do. The Aldens go about most of their adventures with as little adult supervision as possible — something else that delights young readers.

Miss Warner lived in Putnam, Connecticut, until her death in 1979. During her lifetime, she received hundreds of letters from girls and boys telling her how much they liked her books.